PRAISE FOR
INDEH

"INDEH is brilliant. It's an important and tough and beautiful and brutal book. Hawke and Ruth don't flinch in their re-creation of one of our modern continent's most important and mythical creation stories. Please read this important graphic novel. You'll lose yourself in it."

—Joseph Boyden, author of *Three Day Road* and *The Orenda*

"Ethan Hawke and Greg Ruth's INDEH is haunting, powerful, and gorgeous. Every brushstroke, and every word take readers deeper into this often forgotten corner of America's history and into the soul of the Apache people. Easily one of the best graphic novels of the year."

—Jeff Lemire, author of the *Essex County* trilogy

"A crucial book about a fundamental part of our recent history: America's war to subjugate the Apache. Moving and unforgettable, INDEH puts the lie to every movie about the West you have ever seen."

—Philipp Meyer, author of *The Son* and *American Rust*

"Beautiful brushstrokes by Ruth bring the conflict between the Apache and the United States in 1872 to life in a collaboration with actor Hawke that strives to escape Hollywood's western mythos…[T]his respectful approach to America's shameful history is a good start to further a conversation often neglected."

—*Publishers Weekly*

"INDEH, a graphic history by Ethan Hawke and Greg Ruth, is relevant, timely, and appropriate."

—*The Austin Chronicle*

"Seldom has the brutally escalating Apache War—or any war—been depicted with such breathtaking beauty as it is here."

—*Booklist*

A STORY OF THE APACHE WARS

ETHAN HAWKE
GREG RUTH

GRAND CENTRAL
PUBLISHING

NEW YORK   BOSTON

Copyright © 2016 by Ethan Hawke and Greg Ruth
Illustrations copyright © 2016 by Greg Ruth
Foreword copyright © 2016 by Douglas Miles
Afterword copyright © 2016 by Ethan Hawke

Cover design and art by Greg Ruth
Cover copyright © 2017 by Hachette Book Group, Inc.

Grand Central Publishing
Hachette Book Group
1290 Avenue of the Americas
New York, NY 10104
grandcentralpublishing.com
twitter.com/grandcentralpub

Originally published in hardcover and ebook by Grand Central Publishing in June 2016
First Trade Paperback Edition: June 2017

Grand Central Publishing is a division of Hachette Book Group, Inc.
The Grand Central Publishing name and logo is a trademark of Hachette Book Group, Inc.

The publisher is not responsible for websites (or their content) that are not owned by the publisher.

Excerpt from *Neither Wolf nor Dog: On Forgotten Roads with an Indian Elder* by Kent Nerburn. Published by New World Library, Novato, California.

Library of Congress Control Number: 2015960375

ISBNs: 978-1-5387-6006-2 (paperback), 978-1-4555-6410-1 (ebook)

Printed in the United States of America

WOR

10 9 8 7 6 5 4 3 2 1

AN APACHE FOREWORD

Apache culture is very complex. It is a deep blend of belief, ceremony, insight, survival strategy, and social mores that benefit the whole tribe continuously.

For decades American popular culture has attempted to speak for us (Apache) via films, books, and television. Often these stories converge on a road to stereotype, tragedy, pity, savagery, or exploitation. In this book, researched and created by Ethan Hawke and Greg Ruth, the story of the Chiricahua Apache fighting for independence is told again, but from a rare Apache point of view, making this book unique in its creation and purpose.

From the murder of Geronimo's family to the capture of Cochise under truce to the beheading of Mangas Coloradas for sport and "science," *Indeh* pulls no punches, providing readers with an honest account of the desperate and bloody history experienced by the Apache from the 1860s until the surrender of Geronimo.

Indeh comes to life in the fluid brushstrokes that capture the immediacy of the Apache plight, painting a vivid portrait of a people upended and forced to be bold, driven, and wholly at war, yet still remaining very human.

What motivates people to battle the most technically advanced and powerful nation in the world? People assume it is savage violence for its own sake, as so many Hollywood films have interpreted it. Popular culture would have you believe our own innate tribal nobility prompted us on paths to violence. In reality, any time a culture around the world has its way of life threatened, it has fought fiercely to preserve it.

Apache tribes and bands were no different. Apache people were not senseless marauders nor rambling nomads, as anthropology would have us believe, but a people pushed to the brink of violence time and time again due to greed, deception, and the cold blatant racism of the times. *Indeh* provides a rare sympathetic look into the harsh circumstances the Apache people faced during a tumultuous era. What Ethan and Greg have done here is present this to us all in a new and unique way in hopes of bringing a broader understanding of those times, and our own today.

Today xenophobia is at an all-time high. I hope this true story of the Apache Wars serves not only to educate and bring understanding of diverse cultures and human rights, but also to bring about a greater sense of the historical responsibility we all must face for the decisions we make, now and into the future.

Douglas Miles
www.apacheskateboards.com

Douglas Miles Sr. lives and works on the San Carlos Apache Nation. His father, David Miles, was born on the White Mountain Apache Nation and his mother was born on the San Carlos Apache Nation in Arizona. In addition to creating Apache Skateboards, the premier Native-owned skateboard company, Douglas has cast a spotlight on the Apache ethos as a painter, filmmaker, and public speaker, sharing his experiences as a Native artist in America. He's also a fine artist, muralist, filmmaker, and public speaker, and manages the Apache Skate Team.

· PART ONE ·
A BLESSING AND A CURSE

COCHISE IN OJO CALIENTE · SPRING

I did not **pray**...

...nor did I resolve to do **anything** in particular,
for I had no purpose left.

Many of our
people had lost
much in the
massacre...

...but I had
lost **all**.

SEVENTEEN YEARS LATER · MEXICO

Alope and I had been **lovers** for a **long** time before the council granted me the **privilege** to be her husband.

Her father asked for **one hundred** ponies.

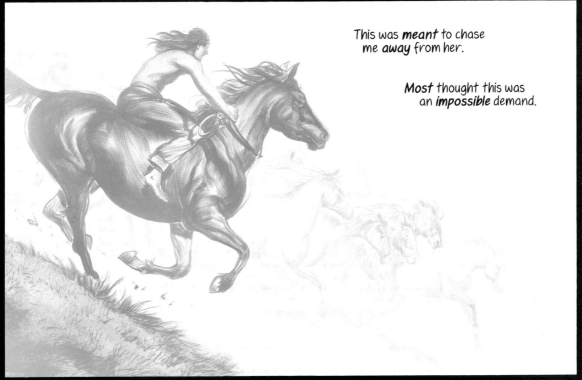

This was **meant** to chase me **away** from her.

Most thought this was an **impossible** demand.

Our *love* was of *no* interest to him.

A few days had passed when I released **one hundred ponies** before his wikiup...

...and **took** with me **Alope**.

14

26

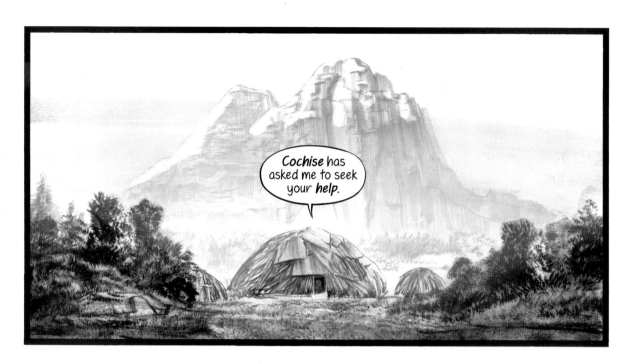

THE CHIRICAHUA APACHE OF CHIEF MANGAS

THE CHIHENNE APACHE OF CHIEF VICTORIO

THE NEDNI APACHE OF CHIEF LOCO

...if *that* is Usen's will.

But it is possible he has *other* plans.

I was *certain* that Goyahkla would find *peace* after the coming battle.

But I was *wrong.*

There would be **no** peace.

Our eyes would set upon a **new** future.

Aiyah, Victorio!

There was no *pity* in it.

No *tears* or *regret* or joy.

Loco!

No **mercy**.

No beating **heart** to **bleed** for what **work** he **must** do.

¡NO!

Por favor, Dios... me libre!

39

I came to **understand** that Goyahkla had **died** back at the camp.

My friend had **burned** there alongside his **family**.

As to **what** he would be **called**...

...*this* I would
know **sooner.**

47

51

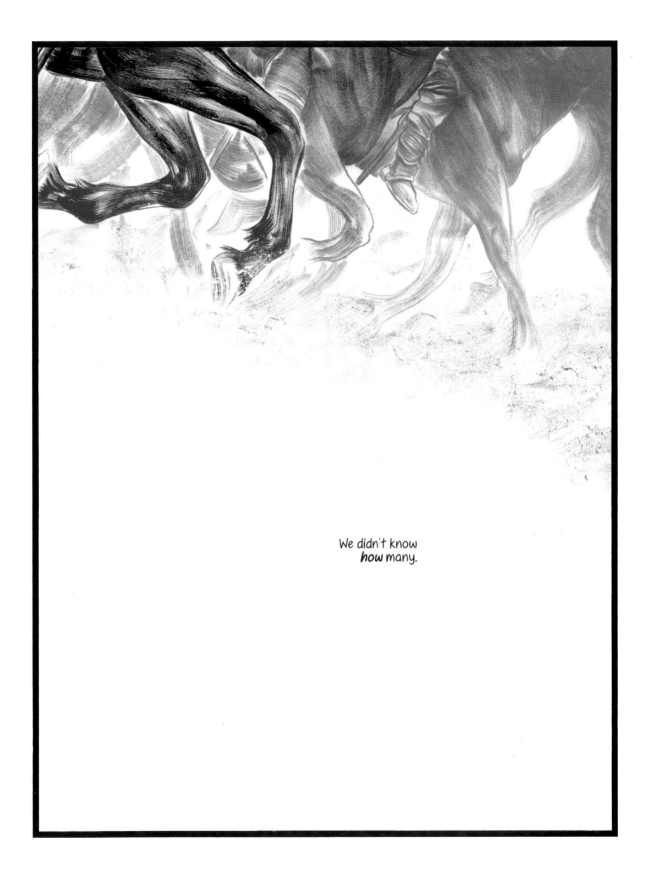

We didn't know
how many.

Most were not
worth counting.

· PART TWO ·
LOCUSTS

The *first* White Eyes we ever saw were to the south of us, near Old Mexico.

We were told they were **measuring** the land to **divide** it up and give it to **other** White Eyes.

I could not **believe** this at the time...

... Let us go and **ask** them.

It was not long before we met more of the White Eyes.

More than we thought possible.

That right there, Bruce?

Yet **another** circumstance where your **money** don't mean **shit**.

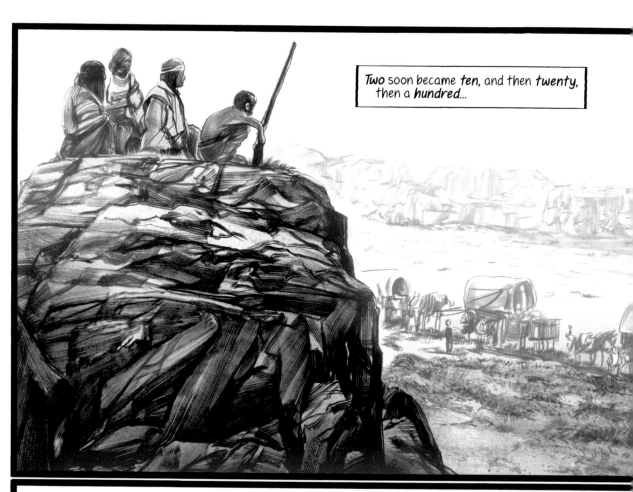

Two soon became ten, and then twenty, then a hundred...

Even so...

They were like a *rain* that fell *everywhere*.

... we had *no* trouble with the *White Eyes*.

TWO YEARS LATER · FORT BOWIE

Sir, I believe he's telling the **truth** about the Ward boy.

I didn't ask **what** you believed, *Lieutenant.*

I do not have them. I have *said* this already.

I *believe* you do *not*.

80

We **have** to let these... *Indians* know we mean *business.*

Colonel ...

... a couple of months ago, some **miners** tied **four** Mescalero Apaches to trees and **bullwhipped** them because they wouldn't tell them where a **gold deposit** was.

Walk with me, *Lieutenant.*

A *dozen* Tontos were *shot* last month up north for *cattle* they *didn't* steal.

The *whole* territory is a *powder* keg.

If we *arrest* one of the *Chiefs* of the Chiricahua, *or* hold his *family* for something he *didn't* do...

Open it.

Yessir!

Colonel Bascom, as you well know, we must bring your savages to heel before the coming winter."

Send the
White Eyes to their
Three-Headed
God.

I see it.

"...and when you get them together, you will kill all the grown Indians."

"Take the children prisoners and sell them to defray the expense of killing the Indians."

"Buy whiskey and such goods as may be necessary to lure and pacify the Indians..."

"Be certain you have a sufficient number of men around to allow no Indian to escape."

"Leave nothing undone to insure success."

105

My warriors want **war**.

Maybe they are **right**.

They are **wrong**, Mangas.

The *Apache* **cannot** win against the *Bluecoats*.

They are **too many**. You **must** make **peace** with them.

This Puppy Nantan, **Bascom**, who **destroyed** our village wants **war**.

I do **not** think we can seek **peace** with him.

Colonel Bascom grows **desperate**, Mangas. There is a **new** nantan coming.

General *Crook*, he is called.

117

TWO MOONS BEFORE WINTER · FORT BOWIE

I have done the **best** I could under the **circumstances,** but...

But... what we have now is **all-out war** with Cochise and likely **all** the other Chiricahua as well.

We have more than one hundred and **fifty** settlers, miners, **and** soldiers **killed** over the past few months...

... without the **death** of a **single** hostile.

We **also** have the *Tontos* and *Yavapais* up north raising hell and **refusing** to come back into the reservation because **your** management has very nearly **starved** them **to death.**

Isn't it *fair* to say that your **best** has **not** been good enough?

122

General,
I have Cochise **all**
but in **hand.**

I... do **not** believe
the other Chiricahua
have joined him, but have
instead **skulked** off to
hide in Mexico.

If the... General will
grant me **one** more company
from the **new** cavalry you
have brought...

... I can give
the citizens of this **great**
territory the **extermination**
of the Chiricahua they so
justly call for.

128

Oh shit.

136

141

You are Mangas Coloradas, are you not?

Yes.

You alone?

I am.

My name is Charles Gatewood. I'm honored to meet you.

Sergeant, tie up his horse. Shelby, get him a cup of coffee.

Why are you here?

Thank you.

I am going to see your General Crook to tell him I want peace with the White Eyes.

I want to take my people back to Ojo Caliente, and live there at war with no one anymore...

... You can take me to your General?

... We recently **fought** against **Cochise** near Tularosa.

Your **Bedonkohe** were there as well. **Bascom**, our nantan, was **killed** and **all** our soldiers, except for the ones **here**.

There **will** be **those** who will want to **kill** you for that.

Will your **General Crook** want to kill me?

I **believe** he **will** listen to what you have to **say**, but I **cannot** guarantee your **safety** at Fort Bowie.

Even so, I **must** go with you.

My **Power** has shown me the Bluecoats in numbers like **grasshoppers**. It told me we **must** bend to the will of the **White Eyes**.

149

153

We ain't *officially* met yet. My name's *Mickey Free*...

... *half* Irish, *half* Apache, and *all* son of a bitch.

Well, now...

The *greatest* wrong ever done to the Apaches was the *betrayal* and *murder* of Mangas Coloradas.

That is the *biggest* guldurned head I *ever* did see!

After that we did not *waste* bullets on the *Mexicans*, or even *arrows*. We killed *them* with rocks, like *rats*.

154

Bullets were for the White Eyes.

155

· PART THREE ·
A THREE-HEADED GOD

161

... And we'll need **hardtack** and two cases of **powder** as well.

I can **outfit** you right enough. Pull your supply mules around **back** where I keep my stores, and we'll get you **loaded**.

I **may** have to disappoint you on the **hard-tack**, though.

Lieutenant **Gatewood**?

Sergeant Gatewood now...

... And *you* are?

Brigadier General Oliver **Howard**, with **orders** from President Grant.

You fell *out* of Mr. Crook's *favor*, I see.

Yessir. He *did* receive those orders *two weeks* back, but he's out up north with a company hoping to *encourage* the Yavapais back to the *reservation*.

Should be back *presently*. Sir.

And your *present* situation?

165

Anyone can
kill an *enemy*...

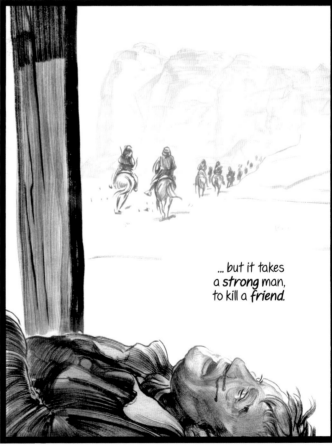

... but it takes
a **strong** man,
to kill a *friend*.

SKELETON CAVE · ARIZONA

That's *Tui*. **Mean** little fucker. *Unreasonable.*

This is *his* way of saying you are full of *shit*, General.

Tell the **chief** one last **damned** time...

... that I do **not** want to **kill** them, but I **will** if they do not **surrender** now and go with me back to the **reservation.**

Lotta work before breakfast, **huh**, General?

I'm **told** your **real** name is **Ward**, and that your **father** started all this god-awful **mess** with the Chiricahua after you were **kidnapped.**

Was it the *Yavapais* that **took** you?

He wadn't my **real** father, and he **made up** all that kidnappin' **bullshit.**

I got **tired** of him **beatin'** on me so I took some **horses** and came up **north.**

My **mother** was Yavapais, so they took me in.

179

Naiches...

181

I don't suppose **you** had **anything** to do with the president's decision, **did** you, Oliver?

I believe the **Lord** allowed me to **contribute** to his thinking.

It **won't** work

George...

... if the **present** approach continues, **you** and the **Chiricahua** will soon be **eating** each other.

You are a **righteous** man, Oliver, so let **me** tell **you** what *I* believe.

I believe that history is **finished** with the Apache.

He and **his** land and **everything** he owns **now** belongs to **us** to dole back out to him as **we** see fit.

183

Then **pray** on your **own**, George, for a clean **heart**.

We **make** history, and we are **damned** or **saved** by how **we** do it.

You **see**, it is **we** who will be damned for **our** heedless **destruction** of **every** buffalo, and of **all** the beautiful grasses and every **red** or **black** man who got between **us** and "**civilization**."

I believe **your** beloved **history** will remember us as a particularly **incorruptible** race of men.

We **white** Americans absolutely **cannot** be bought off from **taking** and **destroying** not just what we **need**, but everything, in the name of **civilizing** it.

George, in accordance with the desires of President Grant, **we** are **no** longer at **war** with **Cochise** or **any** other **Apache** tribe or **band**.

We will *not* beat them into compliance.

We *will* create an atmosphere of *respect* and brotherly *love*...

... and pray that at least this *one* small chapter of history *might* happen as it *should*, rather than as it *tends* to.

I take it I am *relieved*?

President Grant has *transferred* you to South Dakota, where I expect your *abilities* are better suited to the task at hand.

Your friend, Mr. *Gatewood* is to remain *here* to aid me in *mine*.

Charles is more like *you* than I can *stand* at times, but he's a *good* man and I believe he will help you where you *need* it.

But it *chills* my blood to *think* of what you two together might get into *here*.

God *bless* you, George!

187

You are **more** than **half** crazy, Oliver.

Just remember, President Grant **won't** be president **forever**...

... and I am a **patient** man.

I will not put you in an **awkward** place by **disparaging** your **friend**, Mr. Gatewood...

... but there are more men like **him** than there are **not** in this world.

... and **that** is going to make what must be done all the harder... Lieutenant.

If you are trying to buy my **loyalty**, you **needn't**.

I **never** pay for what comes **free** with the job, Mr. Gatewood. I am just a **believer** in clean slates.

Can you take me to **Cochise**?

189

I do *not*, sir, but neither does *she*.

How does she *tell* you anything?

Through *love*! Sun Ya is what we *all* are...

... made *wounded* and *dumb* in this world by the *horrors* it contains, yet *still* capable of *love*.

Hallelujah, thank you, Father!

This is *Naiches*, Cochise's *son* and *heir*.

Good *Lord*, how *long* has he been *back* there?

Since *yesterday* afternoon, making *sure* we were *alone*.

Why didn't you *tell* me?

Heh. I *thought* you *knew*.

192

COCHISE · THE DRAGOON MOUNTAINS

Buenos *dias.*

Then you **will not** go to San Carlos.

I want to see you at a new reservation set up for the *Chiricahua* near *Tularosa*.

If you **agree** to that, we can have peace **now**.

Today.

Tularosa...

Are you prepared to **stay** until I can gather the **other** chiefs?

I will stay for as **long** as it **takes**.

FORTY MOONS AFTER THE MASSACRE AT SKELETON CAVE

We believe there is **no** future for us at *Tularosa.*

My brother, *Juh*, asks me that I speak for **him** as well as **myself.**

Food does **not** stay well upon our stomachs in Tularosa. *Ojo Caliente* is a **good** and **sacred** place to all the Chiricahua.

If we **must** go upon a reservation, why will the Great Father **not** make it **there?**

Because the **white man** has discovered **gold rocks** in the **earth** there, and wants the land for **himself.**

205

All right.

It will be **done**.

I will appoint a **good** man of **my** choosing...

... speaking with **my** voice, as your agent there.

I will honor your treaty with this... **Bluecoat** for as **long** as it **lasts**, but the **Chihenne** will **not** be penned up.

I will take my band to **Old Mexico**.

Victorio is my *chief*.

This one-armed nantan who talks to *Usen* has *much* power.

The Bedonkohe *will* try *peace* with him.

Then it is *done*.

It may feel hot as *Hell* in here, but the *Lord* is in the place, my friends.

When we were **young**, we walked
over this country, **East** and **West**,
and saw **no** other people
than the **Apache**.

After **many** summers, we walked again and found **another** race of people had come to **take** it.

Steady...

How is that?

Why is it the **Apache** now carry their **lives** on their **fingernails**?

We have fought **long** and as **best** we could against you.

We have killed **ten** White Eyes for **every** Apache, but when **one** white man dies, **many** take his place.

When **one** Apache dies, there is **no one** to take **his** place.

As we walked away, our
feet didn't even leave *footprints*.

216

217

It is said the **rattlesnake** is a very **wise** reptile.

He **permits** the prairie dog and his wife to make a nice **warm** nest in the ground...

... and then he **quietly** takes possession of it **without** disturbing its inmates, who are **ignorant** of the snake's **intentions**.

When the prairie dogs have **babies**, the snake **devours** one of the brood from time to time, **but** leaves **no** evidence of it...

... so the parents **never** suspect their **dangerous** friend, who **always** puts on his **best** behavior in their presence.

Then when there are no more **babies**, he eats the **parents** too.

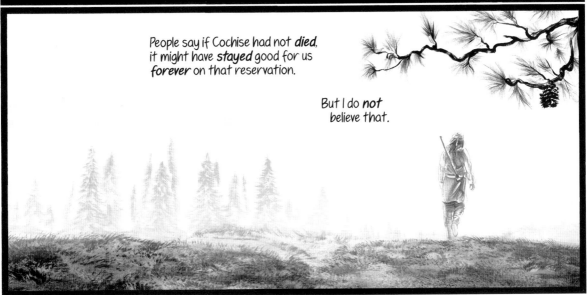

People say if Cochise had not **died**, it might have **stayed** good for us **forever** on that reservation.

But I do **not** believe that.

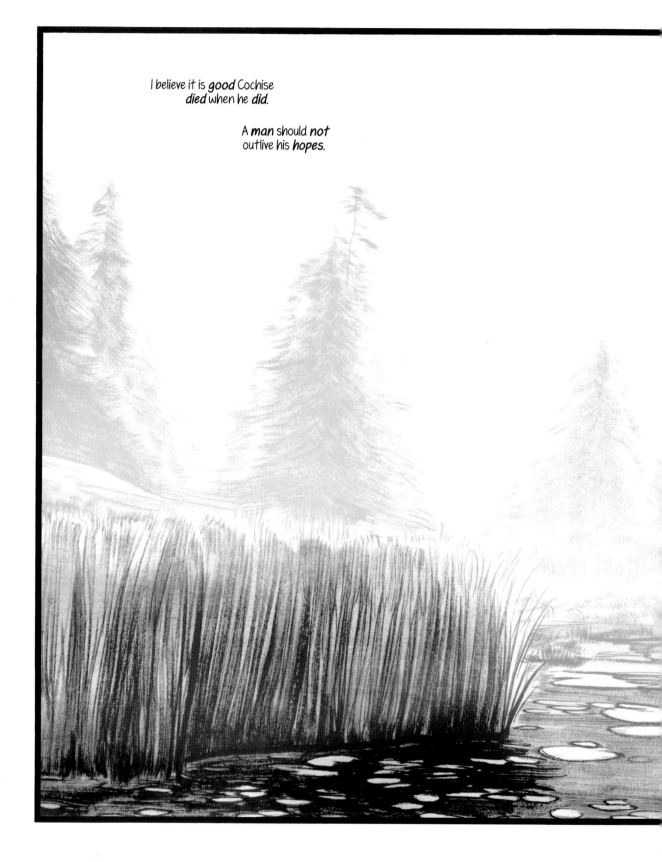

I believe it is **good** Cochise **died** when he **did**.

A **man** should **not** outlive his **hopes**.

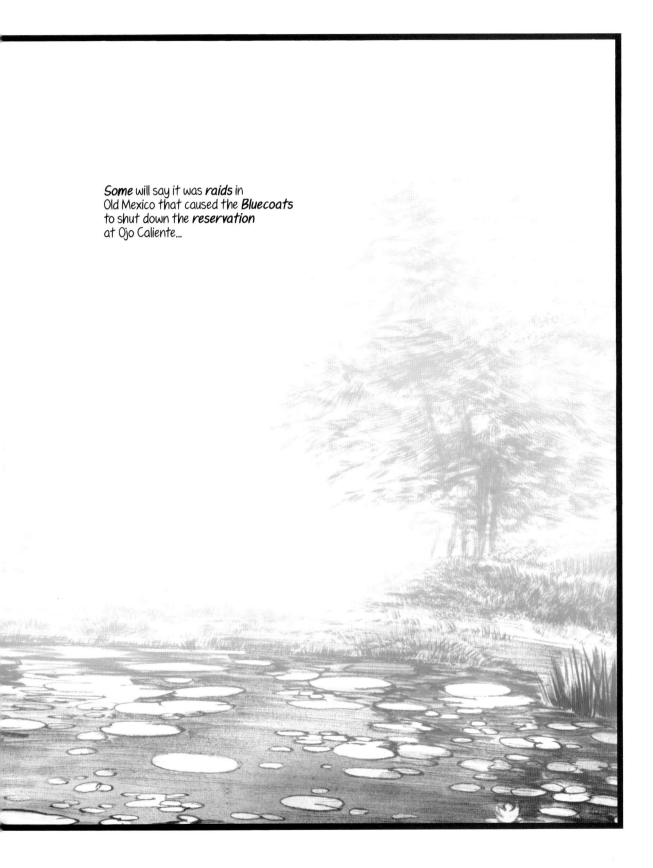

Some will say it was *raids* in
Old Mexico that caused the *Bluecoats*
to shut down the *reservation*
at Ojo Caliente...

... but *that* is just
what the *rattlesnake*
told the *prairie dogs.*

AFTERWORD

Eight years old and sitting in the back of my dad's baby blue Plymouth Barracuda, I engaged my *Star Trek* figures in battle on the armrest. My dad was heartbroken, trying to heal from his divorce by taking me camping in the most remote places he could find. Out in the red dirt along the Arizona–New Mexico border one day, I felt the atmosphere of the car shift. My dad, my real-life Captain Kirk, was suddenly nervous. An old man waved us down from the center of the two-lane road—the only living thing as far as my eyes could see. I heard him say in an unfamiliar cadence, "You are not supposed to be here."

My father apologized. The man came to the window and peered in at me. He was wearing a blue jean tuxedo and had the sort of ancient eyes you'd imagine might belong to a tree.

"You're lucky it's me who found you," he said, looking directly at me.

"What happened?" I asked once we had turned around and were heading away.

My father explained what an Indian reservation was, what an Apache was, how we really shouldn't have been there at all, and how lucky he was not to have gotten his ass kicked. Why were we lucky it was the old man who found us? What did he mean?

My father told me, "Many of the Indians are very angry. And they damn well should be."

"At me?" I asked.

The Barracuda drove on, but the old man's eyes stayed with me. At the roadside shops I started buying books about Geronimo, about Cochise and Victorio and Lozen—anything I could find. Some were mindless, some boring, others full of mystery and power. Abruptly the cowboy movies I'd always loved took on a different hue. They were full of lies. Those gunfights weren't cool, heroic frays—they were slaughters.

Growing up with my mother—back in Vermont, New York, New Jersey—the West held its grip on my imagination. I'd forage libraries for books on

Geronimo as if maybe I could find my dad and me camping in one of them, as if maybe the answer to why the world was so full of treachery might be found somewhere in the Apache story.

Late in my youth and early in my acting career I made a movie in Alaska alongside Native American actors who helped me develop a less juvenile and romanticized view of their history. Eventually I ran across a few films that rang true—*Smoke Signals, Powwow Highway*—and I discovered Sherman Alexie's *The Lone Ranger and Tonto Fistfight in Heaven*, but authentic Native American perspectives were mostly absent from the dominant historical narrative of the Old West.

Years later, by a twist of fate, or because history is prone to repeat itself, I found myself on a canoe trip out west, attempting to recover from my own failed marriage. It was then that I became friends with my guide, the prodigious writer Charles Gaines. He too had a passion for Native American history, and he introduced me to David Roberts's *Once They Moved Like the Wind*, a beautifully crafted account of the Apache Wars. Inspired by the book, we set about writing a film—and my education began in earnest.

Soon I was the divorced dad taking my own kids camping in New Mexico and Arizona. As I researched for our script I was shocked at how much of this pivotal piece of American history remains unknown even to the people who live there. The horrors of genocide sit differently in the mind when you're no longer in the backseat playing with *Star Trek* figures—when it's your turn to drive the car. The more I read about the history of this country and its original human inhabitants, the more I yearned to make the film. The Apache Wars are a vital part of our American history that needs to be told in a way that honestly appreciates and integrates, rather than appropriates, Native American history. The story needs to be told again and again until the names of Geronimo and Cochise are as familiar to young American ears as Washington and Lincoln. I knew that it was not really my story to tell, but my heart felt compelled to tell it.

Geronimo made the perfect protagonist for an epic tale. He was complex—part villain, part victor—a real Shakespearean hero. The script, however, with all Native American leads, was a difficult sell in the star-driven Hollywood marketplace. It would also be extremely costly to shoot. After a few years without any progress in getting the film made, an idea occurred to me one afternoon as my son and I wandered the aisles of Forbidden Planet in New York City: this story might be served better by another medium.

I asked renowned graphic novelist Greg Ruth to read the script. I had been moved by his art, by its powerfully emotional qualities. He liked the script but made it clear that if I was looking for someone to simply storyboard my film script, I had picked the wrong guy—he had too much respect for the form and possibilities of the graphic novel. But if I wanted to dig in and work hard to use this material to build something unique to the medium, he would dig in with me. The writing, poetry, passion, and research of Charles Gaines are also woven throughout the work you hold in your hands now, and Greg and I are both indebted to him.

It has taken a long time for the two of us to complete this project—one of the most mysterious, surprising, and soul-enriching endeavors of my life. I have come across a handful of radical and brilliant artistic minds in my thirty-plus years of acting but no one shines brighter than Greg Ruth. I have learned much about storytelling from him. For the last several years, every few weeks Greg would send me a handful of images and we would write, rewrite, and write again. We have worked on it backstage at my plays, in his studio in Massachusetts, over the phone as we picked up our kids from school, in Albuquerque, and even at the scene of one of the crimes—the original El Rancho Motel, where the cast and crew of the old-time Westerns stayed while they were making their Hollywood fables.

The little boy who scoured roadside souvenir shops so many years ago wanted to know the whole story, and I hope through this book young people like my own son and daughters will gain a deeper understanding of the Apache Wars. It's an important strand in the fabric of our American history.

In the last analysis, we must all, Indian and non-Indian, come together. This earth is our mother, this land is our shared heritage. Our histories and fates are intertwined, no matter where our ancestors were born and how they interacted with each other.
—*Kent Nerburn, Neither Wolf nor Dog*

Ethan Hawke
September 2015

FURTHER READING

Ball, Eve. *In the Days of Victorio*. Tucson: The University of Arizona Press, 2008.

—. *Indeh: An Apache Odyssey*. Norman: University of Oklahoma Press, 1988.

Barrett, S. M. *Geronimo's Story of His Life*. Williamstown: Corner House Publishers, 1989.

Betzinez, Jason. *I Fought with Geronimo*. New York: Bonanza Books, 1959.

Bourke, John G. *An Apache Campaign in the Sierra Madre*. Lincoln: University of Nebraska Press, 1987.

Cremony, John C. *Life Among the Apaches*. Lincoln: University of Nebraska Press, 1983.

Debo, Angie. *Geronimo: The Man, His Time, His Place*. Norman: University of Oklahoma Press, 1976.

Gulbrandsen, Don. *Edward S. Curtis: Visions of the First Americans*, Edison: Chartwell Books, 2006.

Howard, Oliver Otis. *Autobiography of Oliver Otis Howard, Major General, United States Army*. Lexington: Bibliolife, 2010.

Jackson, Clarence S. *William Henry Jackson: Picture Maker of the Old West*, New York: Charles Scribner's Sons, 1947.

Machula, Paul R. *Tale of the Apache Kid*. Globe: 2006.

Marquis, Arnold. *A Guide to America's Indians: Ceremonials, Reservations, and Museums*. Norman: University of Oklahoma Press, 1975.

Miles, Dale Curtis, and Paul R. Machula. *History of the San Carlos Apache*. San Carlos: San Carlos Apache Historic and Cultural Preservation Office, 1997.

Moody, Ralph. *Geronimo: Wolf of the Warpath*. New York: Sterling Publishing Co., 2006.

Nerburn, Kent. *Neither Wolf nor Dog: On Forgotten Roads with an Indian Elder*. Novato: New World Library, 2002.

Opler, Morris Edward. *Myths and Tales of the Chiricahua Apache Indians*. Lincoln: University of Nebraska Press, 1994.

Roberts, David. *Once They Moved Like the Wind: Cochise, Geronimo, and the Apache Wars*. New York: Simon and Schuster, 1994.

Rowe, Jeremy. *Photographers in Arizona 1850–1920: A History and Directory*. Nevada City: Carl Mautz Publishing, 1997.

Scherer, Joanna Cohan. *Indians: The Great Photographs That Reveal North American Indian Life, 1847–1929, From the Unique Collection of the Smithsonian Institution*. New York: Bonanza Books, 1973.

Soens, A.L., ed. *I, the Song: Classical Poetry of Native North America*. Salt Lake City: The University of Utah Press, 1999.

Sonnichsen, C. L. *Geronimo and the End of the Apache Wars*. Lincoln: University of Nebraska Press, 1990.

Sweeney, Edwin R. *From Cochise to Geronimo: The Chiricahua Apaches 1974–1886*. Norman: University of Oklahoma Press, 2012.

Utley, Robert M. *A Clash of Cultures: Fort Bowie and the Chiricahua Apaches*. D.C.: National Park Service Division of Publications, 1977.

—. *Geronimo*. New Haven: Yale University Press, 2012.

Worcester, Donald E. *The Apaches: Eagles of the Southwest*. Norman: University of Oklahoma Press, 1979.